The Super Smelly ALIEN

igloobooks

Down on Mouldy Moon, in a valley made of cheese,
Alvin was playing with his jimpy-jumpy fleas.

This igloo book belongs to:

....

igloobooks

Published in 2015
by Igloo Books Ltd
Cottage Farm
Sywell
NN6 0BJ
www.igloobooks.com

HUN001 0215
2 4 6 8 10 9 7 5 3 1
ISBN 9781-78440-539-7

Illustrated by Kate Leake

Printed and manufactured in China

"Come on," he said, "I'm bored of this place!"
So, Alvin and his fleas zoomed off into space.

At Lunar Lake, Alvin and his fleas landed with a splat,
right in the middle of a cosmic cowpat!

The One-eyed Woggles were covered, head to toe.
"Oh, dear," said the fleas, "we really need to go."

There was a yummy picnic at their next exciting stop.
One alien asked Alvin, "Would you like some galactic pop?"

With a curly, wurly straw, Alvin took a big slurp.
Then, suddenly he let out the most enormous BURP!

Down a black hole they whizzed and whirled.
"Wheee!" said the fleas, as they swirled and twirled.

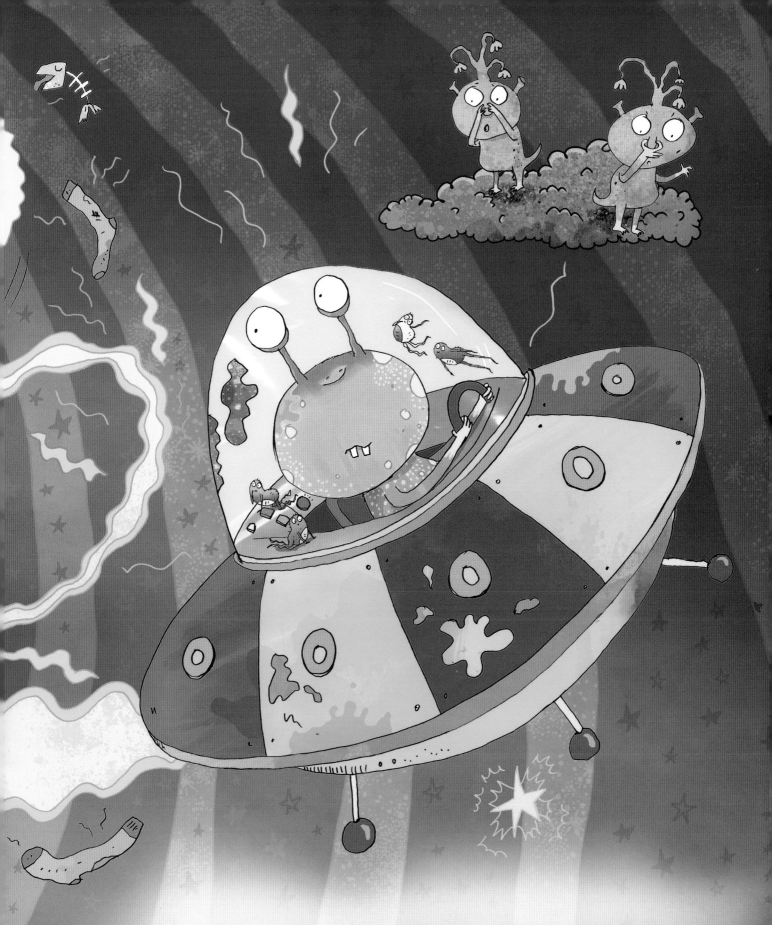

"Don't stop here," said the Piggles, with a scowl.
"The pong from your ship is simply foul!"

"Mmm," said Alvin, "I can smell something yummy.
Let's land at Crunchy Comet and eat something scrummy."

Too many buns made his big tummy grumble.
Then his bottom did a burp that made the ground rumble.

Bursting with pretty perfumes galore,
the next place made Alvin feel worse than before.

The Pufflings covered him in sweet-smelling sprays.
Running off he cried, "I won't smell stinky for days!"

Twisting and turning, they landed safely on the ground.
In Twilight Town, stardust was falling all around.

The dust made Alvin's nose tickle. Suddenly, he went, "Ah-choo!"
He covered the Long-nosed Noodles in green galactic goo.

At Meteor Meadow, the Polettes held their little noses,
as Alvin's super stench killed their daisies and roses.

The aliens shouted, "Take your fleas and go away.
You smell gross. We don't want to play today."

Alvin and his fleas were far from home.
They had made no friends and were all alone.

With tears in his eyes, Alvin took a big sniff,
when he smelled the most delicious whiff.

"This is Planet Pong," the Stinky Snoggles said with glee.
"We'll play with you and your jimpy-jumpy fleas."

With lots of gross smells, stinks, goo and slime,
Alvin and his fleas had the most wonderful time!

"Goodbye, smell you soon!"